Argo & Me

by
Chandra Ghosh Ippen

Pictures by
Erich Ippen Jr.

a story about being scared
and finding protection, love, and home

For the staff and children I knew at Lincoln Children's Center.
You are still in my heart.

Piplo productions
San Francisco, CA
Piploproductions.com

Copyright 2022 © Chandra Ghosh Ippen and Erich Ippen, Jr.

All rights reserved. No part of this book may be reproduced or transmitted in any form or by any means, electronic, or mechanical, including photocopying, recording, or by any information storage and retrieval systems, without prior written permission from the publisher. Exceptions include brief quotations embodied in critical reviews and articles. For inquiries about special use or bulk purchases contact Piplo Productions. (piplo@piploproductions.com)

The publisher, author, and illustrator take no responsibility for the use of these materials. Please review them and determine if they are appropriate for your specific needs. This book is not intended as a substitute for treatment from a mental health provider. The reader should consult with a mental health provider for any symptoms that may need diagnosis or professional attention.

First edition published in 2022

Library of Congress Cataloging-in-Publication data
Names: Ippen, Chandra Ghosh, author. | Ippen, Erich Jr., illustrator.
Title: Argo and Me: A story about being scared and finding protection, love, and home / by Chandra Ghosh Ippen; pictures by Erich Ippen, Jr.
Description: San Francisco, CA: Piplo Productions LLC, 2022. | Summary: A puppy and a child have had multiple homes and tough times. With the help of family, they find safety and love.
Identifiers: LCCN: 2022913547 | ISBN: 978-1-950168-18-7 (hardcover) | 978-1-950168-17-0 (paperback) | 978-1-950168-21-7 (ebook)
Subjects: LCSH Foster home care--Juvenile fiction. | Adoption--Juvenile fiction. | Family--Juvenile fiction. | Dogs--Juvenile fiction. | Post-traumatic stress disorder--Juvenile fiction. | Trust--Juvenile fiction. | Mental health--Juvenile fiction. | BISAC JUVENILE FICTION / Family / Adoption | JUVENILE FICTION / Family / Orphans & Foster Homes | JUVENILE FICTION / Health & Daily Living / Mental Health | JUVENILE FICTION / Social Themes / Emotions & Feelings
Classification: LCC PZ7.1 .I68 Ar 2022 | DDC [E]--dc23

Special thanks to Barbara Ivins for her wise feedback and to Lili Gray, Melissa Brymer, and Mindy Kronenberg for letting their fur family members be a part of our story.

This is Argo.
He's a lot like me.

He likes soft blankets...

...playing in the water...

He's lived in lots of different places...

We don't know EXACTLY what his life was like before US, 'cause he can't tell us with words. He's a dog you know, but Zeze and Paul said that if you watch and listen carefully, Argo will show you what he likes and what scares him.

Who are Zeze and Paul?

Oh yeah, they're Argo's friends from the animal shelter.

When they first met Argo, he was so scared. He wouldn't eat, and he would hide whenever they came in the room. Zeze and Paul sat on the floor and didn't move. They did this for days.

Then one day, Paul started playing harmonica real soft. Argo listened for a while, poked his nose out, and then came and sat right next to them. That was a happy day.

When we first met Argo, Zeze and Paul said it might take time to earn his trust. People had not always been kind. Some people had hurt him, and Argo didn't know that we were different. I told Argo I knew just how he felt.

Some people I lived with before had big problems and didn't always take good care of me.

Sometimes I worried about new people and new places. Sometimes I felt scared and didn't know why.

My family knew we would all need to be patient and show Argo that we are loving and kind. We got him good food.

We played games together, and we watched carefully to learn what scares him, so we could help him feel safe and loved.

Some things, like thunderstorms and loud noises, scare Argo more than most people.

Other things that usually aren't scary, like boots, used to make Argo really worried.

At first, we put all our boots away, but once Argo trusted us, we helped him learn that boots are ok.

It took a while, but it was important, 'cause sometimes you've gotta wear boots.

My family said that some things might scare Argo because they remind him of bad times. I know what they mean.

I used to worry whenever I saw suitcases. They made me think about all the goodbyes and moves I made before.

But now I know that suitcases mean fun trips, and if people go away, they'll come back because we're family.

For Argo, we learned his most scary thing is when we get mad or sad. We think bad moods remind Argo of bad days. When Argo remembers bad times, he feels icky.

Then sometimes, he acts out,

like the time he chewed on Bunkin Baby.

I got so mad. Argo was upset, but I didn't stop.

I was too

MAD!

Later, my family said I had every right to be mad. Bunkin Baby is special, but they wondered if maybe in other places where Argo lived before, when people got mad, bad things happened.

I looked at Argo. He looked scared, sad, and lonely. I decided we should talk it out. "Argo," I said, "it's not ok to chew on family members. I'm mad, but I still love you. I won't hurt you, and I don't want you to be scared of me."

I think Argo understood.

After we made up, we went to the park. Argo loves the park, and so do I. Zeze and Paul were there. They were so happy to see Argo.

Paul played harmonica, and Argo sang along. It's good to see old friends. Even when they're not with us, they live in our hearts.

Argo has so many people who care about him. He's learning that most people are good and kind. He feels safe and loved.

Just like me.

 Chandra combines her love of story and cute characters with her training in clinical psychology. She has spent over 30 years working to support families affected by stress and trauma and has co-authored over 20 publications related to trauma and diversity-informed practice. She hopes this book helps children start conversations about finding love and safety after tough times.

 As a boy, Erich was always interested in cartoons and character design. In his professional career, he has created visual effects for movies like Rango, Harry Potter, The Avengers, Star Wars and many others. He is also a singer, songwriter, music producer and founding member of the local San Francisco band, District 8.

Other books by Piplo Productions

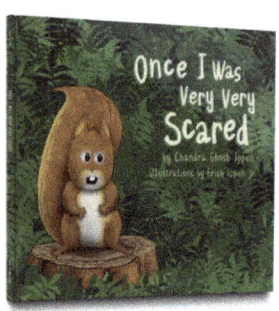
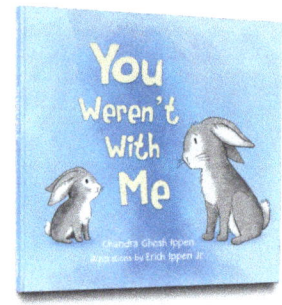

CPSIA information can be obtained
at www.ICGtesting.com
Printed in the USA
LVHW070622280323
742797LV00010B/916